Young Brave
Algonquin

*Illustrations
by M. A. Reardon*

Little, Brown and Company
Boston · Toronto

Young Brave
Algonquin

by

Priscilla Carden

jC1784

Published simultaneously in Canada
by Little, Brown & Company (Canada) Limited

PRINTED IN THE UNITED STATES OF AMERICA

Contents

Young Brave Algonquin

I

Danger!

WAR CRY, the big tawny Indian dog, smelled danger. He stood alert on the riverbank, his glowing yellow eyes fixed on the wooded shore opposite. A growl rumbled in his throat.

It was a sunny morning in autumn, 1658. The forest was sweet with the fragrance of pine and cedar, balsam and juniper. Yellow leaves sailed on the light east wind that blew across the river. On the western bank, behind the dog, there was an open glade.

Four children were playing in the glade. They belonged to a small Algonquin tribe, the Blue River Indians.

[3]

The three boys were shooting arrows at a clam-shell target. The little girl sat frolicking with her pet, a baby beaver.

An overturned war canoe lay nearby.

Farther back, out of sight behind the wooded ridge, stood the low bark wigwams of the village.

Young Brave let fly. *Crack!* The clam-shell target flew to pieces. "War Cry!" he shouted. "Fetch my arrow!"

Nervously, the big dog glanced around. But he did not obey.

There was danger in the air, and War Cry knew it. As best he could, he was warning his young master.

"What's the matter with you?" And Young Brave came running down to look at his dog.

He was an Algonquin boy, dark-faced and bright-eyed. His young body was straight and slim — too slim, for the tribe was short of food. He wore shabby brown deerskin clothes. A hawk feather sprang jauntily from the worn leather band around his head.

"What is it, War Cry? Are you afraid of the river? It makes a lot of noise, doesn't it?"

There had been heavy rains lately, and today the Blue River was in flood. It raced swiftly southward, sparkling and roaring between its rocky banks.

With a laugh, Young Brave fondled his dog. "Don't worry! I won't take you canoeing today!"

[5]

But War Cry did not respond. He stared stubbornly across the river. Memories were coming to him on the wind, memories of last year, of battle, flames and smoke. A long snarl of fear and hate broke from him.

Young Brave stiffened. What was his dog telling him? He looked carefully at the other shore of the river.

He saw a sunny forest, a blackened clearing, distant hills. Beyond those hills lay the towns of the white men. On that blackened clearing the wigwams of his tribe had stood last year, before the white men burned them. The sunny forest was just as usual. Or was it?

Somewhere over yonder, a jay was screaming. Why? And crows were flying up by twos and threes — no, by tens and twenties! A whole flock was taking to the air. What had disturbed them?

"Indians wouldn't frighten the birds," thought Young Brave. "Indians wouldn't travel by day.

White men are coming! But maybe it's only a party of hunters."

Something flashed on the forest slope above the clearing.

"What was that?"

Again the flash came, long and bright, the blinding flash of sunlight on polished metal.

Young Brave turned cold. "It's the sun on a steel helmet! The dog was right! Those are no hunters. A war party is coming." He whirled, holding up both hands. "Danger!" he called. "Hide!"

The Indian children were well trained. No questions were asked. Cricket, the little girl, caught up her pet beaver and scuttled into the underbrush. Keego, the older boy, swiftly gathered up the scattered arrows and dove out of sight. And Dandelion, Young Brave's best friend and adopted brother, came racing toward him.

"This way!" cried Young Brave.

He ran into a thick clump of young pines on the

riverbank. War Cry sprang after him, and Dandelion followed. Both boys flung themselves flat, the dog between them.

"What's the matter?" whispered Dandelion.

"There are white men across the river! War Cry got the scent."

"Hunters?"

"Not hunters. I saw the flash of a helmet. It's a war party!"

"Another war party!" Dandelion flushed with anger. "Can't they let us alone? Haven't they done enough harm to us Indians?"

Just for a second, Young Brave's dark eyes lighted with a smile. It always pleased him when Dandelion spoke of himself as an Indian. For Dandelion, his adopted brother, was not an Indian at all. He was white, with blue eyes and a fair skin. His hair was yellow, bright yellow like the flower for which the Indians had named him.

Six years before, Dandelion had been captured in war. It happened this way.

Chief Arrow Maker, Young Brave's father, had been leading a raid on one of the English towns beyond the hills. While setting fire to a field of corn, he had heard a very small cough. The cough seemed to come from a corn shock which had begun to smolder. Pulling it apart, the chief discovered a small English child sitting within it. The child had looked up at him calmly, showing no

fear. Now, Arrow Maker's own son was about the same age. He decided to adopt this courageous little English boy. He carried him home to his wigwam.

"Look," Arrow Maker had said to Young Brave, "here is your new brother!"

From that day on, the two boys had been the best of friends. They had hunted together, fished together, starved and feasted together. What belonged to one belonged to the other. War Cry, the big tawny dog, had two masters. But he never had to choose which to follow. His masters were always together.

After six years, Dandelion no longer spoke English. He seemed to have forgotten his language, his home and family. Just the same, he was not quite like an Algonquin boy.

"Why are they coming back?" he repeated, his blue eyes sparkling with anger. "Didn't they burn our village last year? Didn't we move across the river to get away from them? And haven't we been hungry ever since? What more do they want?"

To Dandelion, the war was an outrage. He thought it should be stopped — somehow or other! But to Young Brave, it was only a part of the nature of things — a bad part, like cold or hunger. All his life, his people had been fighting with the English.

He said wonderingly, "Why, the war still goes on! Our warriors haven't given up. Don't you remember, last winter they went on snowshoes and burnt a farmhouse. That must be why the white men are coming back — for revenge!"

"But when is this going to end?" muttered Dandelion.

"I suppose it will never end," said Young Brave, sighing. "Not while we can still fight!" And he thought sadly of the change in his people.

Long ago, when Young Brave's grandfather was a child, all this beautiful land of the Northeast had belonged to the tribes of the Algonquins. When his father was a child, white men had be-

gun to arrive in their winged ships. They needed land, more and more land. The Algonquins, friendly at first, began to fight. The white men fought back, and their medicine was very strong. A whole tribe was wiped out. Others retreated.

Young Brave's tribe fled to the Blue River, the ancient boundary of their hunting grounds. Farther they dared not go, for the western bank belonged to another and larger tribe. Yet last fall, after the burning of their village, they had crossed the river. Now they were trespassing on land that was not theirs. They scarcely dared hunt, except close to the river. Often they went hungry.

The wigwams were few now. Only thirty-five warriors remained in the once proud tribe of the Blue River Indians. But the English towns were stronger than ever. Yearly the great ships brought new white men from over the sea to fill up the ranks of the enemy.

"How long will we be able to fight?" asked Dandelion.

But Young Brave had no answer.

Pine needles rustled behind them. Cricket came crawling up, pushing her baby beaver ahead of her. The beaver did not want to be pushed. It wailed like a child. "Hush, hush!" said Cricket.

She was Young Brave's sister, a merry, brown, musical little girl, usually humming to herself. "Sister hums like a cricket!" Young Brave had said years before, and that is how Cricket got her name.

But she was not humming now. Looking very grave, she nestled down beside him and took the beaver into her arms. "Why must we hide?" she whispered.

"Because of white men!'

"White men?" said another voice. And Keego joined the others in the pine clump. He was a tall, strong boy of fourteen, much given to boasting, but capable in many ways. Young Brave felt glad to see him. Surely Keego would know just what to do. And Keego, when he heard the story, was of the same opinion.

"It's a lucky thing I happened to be here, Young Brave! Just leave everything to me. For the present, we must watch and wait!"

"Yes, Keego!"

Silently, the four children peered through the screen of pine boughs.

Young Brave's heart pounded like a war drum. What was going to happen?

On the other shore, the jay had stopped screaming. The crows had all flown away. Spots of color moved among the trees above the clearing. Through the rush and roar of the river, sounds came faintly — the clink of arms, the tramp of feet, the crash of breaking branches.

A man stepped into the clearing. The sunlight fell full on him. He was a white man, tall and fair, with a scarlet cloak falling from his broad shoulders. A high, narrow helmet glittered on his head. He had a ruddy face, light eyes, and a pointed yellow beard. He carried a musket in his hands, ready to fire. Cautiously, he looked all around the clearing.

Young Brave held his breath.

"He's puzzled," whispered Keego. "He thought he'd find our new village on the same spot as the

[15]

old one. He doesn't know we've moved across the river. Ha ha, we fooled him!"

"Hush!" whispered Young Brave.

Just as if he had heard Keego's words, the white man walked down to the clearing's edge and stared across the river.

"He's looking at us!" moaned Cricket.

"No, no," said Young Brave. "He can't see us. But what is he looking at?"

As if satisfied, the white man turned away. He shouted a command.

"Now the others will come!" said Keego. "That man is their chief. They call him the Captain. My father told me about him. He has a farm in one of the towns yonder, and a trading post too. Other Algonquins trade with him, but not our tribe! See, what did I tell you?"

Men began marching into the clearing. They wore tall hats and long cloaks. They carried muskets.

The English war party had arrived.

2

The English
War Party

MARCHING in single file, the white men advanced down the clearing. They were farmers by occupation, but they had been well drilled. They drew themselves up in a long line, facing their Captain and the river. Another line formed behind the first, and another behind that. The clearing filled fast. And still the white men came on, marching steadily out of the forest.

Was there no end to them?

Fearfully, Young Brave watched. He could feel his dog shivering beside him. He darted a look at the other children.

Dandelion was counting the soldiers. He wore his "danger face" — that is what Young Brave called it — a special bright, cool, pleasant and alert look which he always put on when some great danger threatened. Cricket looked frightened. Even Keego, the confident, seemed uneasy. Catching Young Brave's eye, he muttered, "The towns mean business this time! They've never sent such a large force before."

"Not last year?"

"Last year they sent seventy men."

Young Brave too began to count.

Dandelion whispered, "How many?"

"About two hundred."

"That's what I make it. And we have thirty-five warriors!"

All the soldiers had now arrived. They stood rigid in their lines, men in blue cloaks, brown cloaks, green cloaks; clean-shaven men; men with pointed beards. Under their tall, broadbrimmed hats, their eyes gazed sternly ahead. The massed muskets bristled like a grove of young pine trees.

The Captain began to speak.

"Brother," whispered the little girl, her voice trembling, "I don't like to see so many soldiers with guns! Please run back to the wigwams and tell our warriors to come here right away."

The three boys looked at each other.

"Why don't you do as I say?" faltered Cricket.

"Because the warriors aren't there," said Young Brave gently. "They've all gone down the river in the canoes. This is the day of the great hunt, don't you remember? They started as soon as it was light. Dandelion and I saw them off. They were laughing and joking —" He stopped. Something like a sob rose in his throat.

The evening before, a game scout had brought good news. He had found a herd of deer in the cedar swamp several miles down river on the western bank. Deer meant food for the hungry Algonquins. It meant new hunting shirts, robes,

[21]

moccasins, bowstrings, thongs, sewing thread,
bone tools.

How happy and busy they had all been! The
children had rushed about joyously, gathering
wood for the cooking fires. The men had tested
bows, mended arrows. The women had been bus-
iest of all, for they must do the skinning and cooking and tanning. How they had chattered, as they

made ready! Young Brave's mother, Morning Star, had looked so happy!

In the morning, as dawn streaked the sky, the warriors had trooped down to the water's edge. Flood or no flood, the hunt could not wait. Gaily they had launched their birchbark canoes on the pale, roaring river and departed, calling jokes to each other. By now, they were scattered far and wide through the cedar swamp.

"Did they all go?" asked Cricket. "Even the old men?"

"Yes! There are only women and children and sick people in the wigwams."

The little girl began to cry. She cried noiselessly, big tears running down her cheeks.

"Why is she crying?" said Keego angrily. "We're safe, aren't we? The soldiers will never find our new village. Look, they're taking their ease! After a while, they'll march home again."

The Captain had dismissed his men. They broke ranks, sat down, and opening their food pouches, began to eat. The Captain did not sit down. Glancing keenly about at the forest, he shouted a name.

"What's he up to?" whispered Dandelion.

"I don't know," said Young Brave.

Again the Captain shouted, more impatiently this time. And now a startling thing happened. An Indian warrior slipped from the trees and joined him.

The Indian was short and powerful, with a broad face painted for war. He was dressed in deerskins. He carried a bow. On his head he wore the feathers of the Blue River Indians.

"Why, he's one of us!" gasped Young Brave. "But I don't know him!"

"I do!" Keego gave a loud grunt of scorn. "It's Wolf Man, the runaway!"

Wolf Man? A queer shiver ran through Young Brave. What had he heard about Wolf Man? "What did he do, Keego? Didn't the old men sentence him to death?"

"I don't remember about that," said Dandelion.

"No," said Keego. "It happened before you came. I was a little boy then. Wolf Man wasn't like the other warriors. When he got angry, he was dangerous. We children used to hide from him. One day he killed another warrior, one of our own tribe. No one knew what to do. The old men talked all night. In the morning they said he must die. But Wolf Man had run away. We heard he went to live with the white men. Now he has come back!"

"He's helping our enemies, isn't he?" said Cricket. "He must be a very bad man!"

"He's a renegade!" said Keego.

"He's a coward too!" remarked Dandelion. "He let the Captain go ahead and do the scouting. Did you notice?"

Young Brave said nothing. But he shivered again as he watched the squat figure across the river. Wolf Man seemed horrible to him. First he had murdered one of his own people, and now he

[25]

was guiding the enemy against them. Surely such a man would meet a bad end!

The two men had been consulting. Now they moved toward the riverbank. The Captain halted, pointing straight across the river. Wolf Man smiled.

"What is he smiling about?" said Dandelion uneasily. "Have they sighted something on this bank?"

"Nonsense!" said Keego. "We're hidden, and the wigwams are hidden. There's no smoke rising, because the women had nothing to cook. As for the glade, it's empty. I picked up all the arrows myself!"

Young Brave started. A picture came into his mind, a picture of a huge, yellow-stained war canoe lying overturned in the glade. He felt sick.

"What's the matter?" whispered Dandelion.

Young Brave muttered, "The war canoe!"

"What?"

"The war canoe!"

They looked silently at each other.

Keego said, "What's this? What's this?"

"Why, the war canoe is in plain sight! It's given us away!" said Dandelion. "The Captain had only to look at it to know that we've moved over here! Right now he's probably asking Wolf Man how to get across the river."

"Oh!" moaned Cricket.

"Well, they can't get across," said Keego triumphantly, after a pause. "They haven't any boats!"

Dandelion said, "What about the ford?"

"Oh, the ford! Don't worry about that!" cried

Keego. "It's miles down the river, past the cedar swamp, almost to the Singing Water. The white men will never find it."

Young Brave said bitterly, "Haven't they a guide? Look, look there! Wolf Man is betraying us!"

The renegade stood with outstretched arm, pointing down the river. He was talking fast. The Captain cut him short. Running back to his men, he shouted a command. They sprang up and formed their lines as before. He spoke to them briefly. Then, beckoning to Wolf Man, he plunged into the forest on the south. The renegade trotted after him. The soldiers began to follow.

"They're taking our old trail to the ford!" cried Dandelion.

Young Brave felt dazed. Just a few minutes before, the river had protected him. Now it protected him no more. The soldiers would cross by the ford, march up the western bank, and fall on the helpless village. And then? He remem-

bered the story of the Pequots. The Pequots had
been another Algonquin tribe, much larger and
stronger than the Blue River Indians. They too
had defied the white men. Now they were gone.
Would the same thing happen to his tribe?

What was to be done?

He watched numbly as the soldiers left the
clearing. Line after line marched out. They were
all gone now. The long file wound away down
the riverbank and out of sight.

With one accord, the children sprang to their
feet.

"What shall we do?" cried Dandelion.

"We must make a plan!" cried Young Brave.

Keego looked from one to the other, his black
eyes snapping. "There's only one thing to do. We
must make a signal smoke and summon back our
warriors!"

3

The Quarrel
with Keego

"YOUNG BRAVE, get some dry wood immediately! Dandelion, you get the green wood! Cricket, run back to the wigwams as fast as you can and tell all the people to hide in the forest! I'll make the fire!" shouted Keego.

The two boys sprang to obey. The little girl set off at a run, carrying her baby beaver.

Keego ran out into the center of the glade. He cleared away the dead leaves to make a space for his fire. He saved a few for tinder, crumbling them in a little pile. Then he squatted down, drawing his two fire sticks from the pouch at his belt. One was a long, pointed cedar stick, like an arrow. The other was a flat slab of cedar with a pit in the center. He placed the long stick upright on the slab, the point resting in the pit. He looped the string of his bow around the long stick. He held a pine knot on top to steady it. Then he drew his bow back and forth, making the long stick twirl rapidly. Faster and faster it twirled, its sharp point grinding into the pit. Soon the pit was filled with smoking wood dust.

Keego stopped twirling. He blew on the wood dust, and it glowed red. Shaking the red coal into the tinder, he blew carefully. Little flames sprang up.

The fire was made.

"Now the dry wood!" cried Keego.

"Here you are." Young Brave threw down a big pile of sticks and branches. He dashed off to find more. It was good to move fast, to race through the forest with his dog bounding after him. His mind was clear now. The dazed feeling had passed away. Returning with a second load of wood, he added it to the pile and sat down cross-legged to watch Keego. Suddenly he asked, "Why are you calling back the warriors?"

"That's a foolish question!"

"Is it?"

"Of course it is! The white men are marching to the ford, aren't they? Soon they'll be crossing the river."

"Yes, they'll be crossing the river — two hundred of them," said Young Brave slowly.

"Well, that's why our warriors must come back!"

"To fight the white men?"

"Yes."

Young Brave said, "We have thirty-five warriors. Who will win?"

"Will you stop asking questions?" shouted Keego. "Can't you see I'm busy?" He threw a green stick on the fire. A white curl of smoke began to drift skyward.

Young Brave was silent. To himself he said, "The white men will kill our warriors. They will burn our wigwams. They will hunt down the rest of us, sell us as slaves far across the sea! That's what they did to the Pequots! All this will happen if the white men cross the river. Why do we let them cross?"

A plan came to him, a wonderful plan. If he

had been an English boy, he would have shouted for joy. He was Algonquin, so he remained silent. His dark face lighted with a smile. Surely Manitou, the Great Spirit, had sent this plan to him! Breathing quickly, he rose to his feet. War Cry, who had been lying beside him, also stood up, looking at him inquiringly.

"While you've been asking questions," said Keego, "I've made the best signal fire that ever was! Just look at it! Now I need more green wood."

Dandelion rushed up, waving a leafy branch. "Here you are, Keego! It's green, I cut it from the tree with my stone knife!"

Young Brave said, "Give that to me!" Seizing the branch, he walked up to the fire and knocked it apart with a hard blow.

Keego leaped up with a shout.

"What are you doing?" cried Dandelion.

Vigorously, Young Brave began to beat out the flames.

"Stop that, or I'll make you!" Keego made a rush at him. Without a sound, War Cry slipped in front of his young master and stood on guard. His fur bristled; his eyes were cold. Keego stopped short. "Dandelion," he cried, "call off your dog!"

"Can't!" said the English boy mischievously. "He's Young Brave's dog too!"

There was silence as Young Brave finished putting out the fire. He stamped the embers into the ground with his moccasined feet. The last curl of smoke sank and was gone. Throwing down the branch, he folded his arms and faced Keego.

The older boy's face was twisted with rage. "Why did you put out my signal fire?"

"Because it was a mistake! We mustn't make a signal fire."

"Is that so? Then how are we to call back the warriors?"

"We mustn't call them back!"

Keego cried mockingly, "The boy is crazy! The enemy is coming, and he doesn't want the warriors here to defend us!"

"That's just it," said Young Brave calmly. "They can't defend us — not here at the village."

"Then where can they defend us?"

"At the ford," said Young Brave.

Keego opened his mouth, and shut it again.

"Go on, brother!" cried Dandelion, dancing with excitement.

Young Brave continued earnestly, "They must

fight at the ford, don't you see? They must try to stop the enemy from crossing the river! And maybe they can do it! Men in the water are helpless. Numbers don't count. Anyway, it's our only chance!"

Dandelion gave a whoop of joy. "Brother, you're right! Why didn't I think of that?"

There was a flash in Keego's dark eyes that showed he too understood the value of the plan. But his pride was hurt. He turned away sullenly.

Young Brave ran after him. "Wait, wait, Keego! Don't go! We need you! Without you, how could we manage the boat?"

"Boat? What are you talking about?"

"Why, we must take a message to our warriors at once! There's no time to lose, so we must go by water—by boat!"

"The boats are gone," grunted Keego. "All of them. The warriors took them to the cedar swamp."

Young Brave said, "One boat is still here." And he ran to the war canoe and laid his hand on it. "We'll take this one!"

Keego stared at him. "Now I know you're crazy! Why, that's the war canoe! It's too big. You and Dandelion couldn't handle it."

"There are three of us," pleaded Young Brave. "And you're big and strong. With you paddling stern, I think we can manage!"

"But I won't paddle stern!"

"What?"

"I won't go with you! You spoiled my signal fire," burst out Keego. "You're younger than I am, and you have no name! You are just called Young Brave, which means nothing! I'm fourteen, and I've earned a name of honor for myself — Keego the Fish, because I'm a better swimmer than the rest of you. But you think you know best. All right! Carry out your plan! But I won't help you."

Tears of vexation sprang to Young Brave's eyes.

He blinked them away resolutely. Young as he was, he knew that this was no time for a quarrel. Turning away without a word, he studied the war canoe.

It was long and large, a giant birchbark canoe stained yellow with alder juice. A wolftail hung at the stern. On either side of the bow a wide-open black and white eye had been painted. The nearest eye gazed at him fiercely, as if to say, "Young Brave, do you know me? I am the war canoe! Will I obey such a small warrior?"

"Paddle stern yourself!" shouted Keego.

Young Brave drew a long breath. "I will!"

"And I'll paddle bow for you!" cried Dandelion, scowling at Keego.

"Thank you, brother!"

"What a crew!" sneered Keego. "I wonder what will happen to you. The river's in flood, don't forget! And there are rapids downstream, not to mention the Singing Water!"

"Oh, the Singing Water!" cried Dandelion,

with a laugh. "We'll take good care to stay away from that!"

Young Brave did not laugh. Once he had seen a boy carried over the waterfall known as the Singing Water. He had never forgotten this sight, nor the mourning afterward, nor the burial of the drowned boy. Ever since, he had felt a secret fear of the Singing Water. Still, it was far away, past the cedar swamp, even past the ford. Manitou would help him! He said resolutely, "Come on, brother! Let's launch our canoe."

Seizing the great canoe, they turned it over. Gently they drew it through the leafy glade and down to the riverbank.

"Good-by!" shouted Keego. "I'm going back to the wigwams now to tell everybody to run far, far away! Because of you, there won't be any warriors to defend them!"

He ran swiftly up the slope and disappeared.

Splash! The war canoe dropped into the water. Young Brave grasped the stern while Dandelion leaped in and ran up into the bow. Then he too leaped in. Just as the current whirled them away, a tawny body flashed through the air and landed with a *thud* in the center of the canoe.

"War Cry!" exclaimed Young Brave.

The dog settled down meekly, his muzzle on his forepaws. His yellow eyes shone with happiness. "You didn't think

I would stay behind, did you?" he seemed to say.

"So there are three of us after all!" laughed Young Brave. "Even without Keego!"

"I'd rather have the dog," said Dandelion. "He isn't afraid."

Both boys drew paddles from the buckskin loops along the inner sides of the canoe. They raised their paddles high.

"To the cedar swamp!" shouted Young Brave, as he had heard his father do that morning.

"To the cedar swamp!" echoed Dandelion.

The two paddles dipped together. And so the voyage began.

4

Sign Language

"STOP, STOP!" A woman was running down from the wigwams to the riverbank. It was Morning Star, Young Brave's mother. Cricket was with her. "Come back, boys!"

"We can't, Mother!" called Young Brave. "White men are marching to the ford! We must tell our warriors!"

Morning Star clasped her hands. "But the rapids! Keego says you'll be drowned!"

"Manitou will help us!"

"Watch out!" cried Dandelion suddenly.

The main current hit them, flinging them sideways. They nearly went over. Cricket screamed. Paddling furiously, the two boys at last managed to head the bow downstream with the current. Now the big canoe ran on smoothly and swiftly, keeping balance with the ease of a waterbird.

"What a boat!" panted Dandelion.

And Young Brave felt a thrill of pride, remembering that only the Indians of the Algonquin tribes knew the art of building the birchbark canoe. "Can't do much but steer," he answered.

"That's all," agreed Dandelion. "But anyway, the river is taking us where we want to go."

"Yes," thought Young Brave, "but what will happen to us after we get there?"

Morning Star did not call again. Looking back, they saw that Cricket had run to her and had hidden her face in her mother's soft deerskin robe. Morning Star, her arms around the child, stood gazing intently at the canoe. Cricket's pet, the little beaver, sat on his haunches beside her, also watching. Then the canoe whirled around a bend, and the little group was hidden from sight.

The boys paddled in silence for some time. The Blue River was changed, on this day of flood. Close attention was needed. Logs and uprooted trees traveled with them. The current ran with unusual speed and force. Even the shore line was different, for here and there floodwater had run back among the trees, drowning familiar landmarks.

They saw nothing of the white men. Anxiously,

Young Brave asked himself: "How far ahead are they? Did we start too late? Can we give our warning to the warriors in time?"

War Cry lay quietly in the bottom of the boat. He did not sleep, and presently he raised his head and seemed to listen.

Young Brave listened too. He heard a hoarse, low roar. It was the sound of breaking water — the sound of the rapids.

Surely they had not come so far as this in such a short time? But they had. As they swept around the next bend, they saw white water ahead of them.

Even in ordinary times, these rapids were dangerous. Indians usually portaged around them. Today there was no time for a portage. And the river was in flood. What would happen?

"If we capsize," thought Young Brave, "who will take our message to the warriors?" He threw down his paddle. "Brother," he cried, "let's pray to the Great Spirit!" Rising, he held out both arms

to the blue sky in the Indian fashion. "Manitou,
O Great Spirit, Your Indians are in danger today!
Look down and help us! Guide us two boys safely
through the rapids!"

Dandelion did not rise. Listening gravely, he
seemed to remember something from the far-off

time when he lived with his own people. He bowed his head, saying a word that was not an Indian word: "Amen!"

They went on paddling. Now the river narrowed and the speed of the current increased. The shores rose on either hand in rocky cliffs topped with oaks. Black rocks and white foam filled the gorge ahead. The roaring noise was very loud. War Cry stood up, looking uneasily at his master.

"Lie down and don't move!" commanded the boy.

The dog obeyed. Shivers ran over his shaggy body.

With a shudder, with a wild sidelong swing, the war canoe plunged into the rapids.

"*Yi-yi-yi-yi-yi!*" shouted Young Brave, giving his war whoop as he had heard his father do when entering some dangerous stretch of water. From the bow Dandelion also cried out, "*Yi-yi-yi-yi-yi!*"

"Wow, wow!" barked War Cry.

Two rocks loomed ahead, with a glistening channel between them. With all his strength Young Brave steered for the channel. They shot down it with fearful swiftness, plunged into foam, and dashed on. Young Brave, shaking the water from his face, paddled grimly. Dandelion's short, quick strokes never faltered. Sometimes tossing like a birch leaf, sometimes darting like an arrow from a strong man's bow, the great canoe rode the rapids. Dimly, Young Brave realized that the flood was helping them. Because the water was so high, many dangerous rocks were safely covered.

Suddenly it was all over. The roaring dropped, the river widened, the cliffs sank. The battered war canoe floated on smooth, swift water as before. Two exhausted boys paused to smile at each other. And War Cry, whimpering aloud now that the danger was over, crawled up to lick his master's hand.

"The Great Spirit heard your prayer," said Dandelion.

"Yes," said Young Brave. "Look, there is the cedar swamp!"

On the western bank of the river lay a dark green lowland, dotted with blue pools. This was the cedar swamp, where the men of the tribe had come that morning to hunt deer. A heron was wading slowly through a pool. Two hawks hung almost motionless overhead. Red-winged blackbirds called sweetly.

Not a hunter was in sight. And the current would soon carry them past.

"Shall we call out?" whispered Dandelion.

"Better not! The English war party can't be far away."

"Perhaps we've passed them!"

"I don't think so," said Young Brave, staring at the other bank. There too the ground was swampy, and the trail to the ford swung back into the oak forest. He saw no sign of his enemies.

If they were still moving at the same pace, they were probably somewhere ahead.

"White men hear nothing," said Dandelion with scorn. "Let's call."

"But Wolf Man is with them!"

"That's so. Well, let the dog signal for us!"

"All right." Young Brave turned back to the cedar swamp. Before he could give the signal, a great buck rose from cover and sprang away over the swamp with tremendous bounds.

"Look, look! How he jumps!" cried Dandelion. "What frightened him?"

Young Brave's eyes flashed. "Who shot him, you mean! He won't get far!"

Just as he spoke, the deer fell suddenly and lay still. An Indian warrior stepped from a clump of cedar and ran forward, a bow in his hand. He was tall and gaunt, dressed in worn deerskins. A birchbark quiver was slung at his back. About his neck hung a pouch in which he carried his war paints. Long feathers jutted from his black scalp lock.

Young Brave said to himself, "Manitou is still with us!"

The warrior was Arrow Maker, his father, chief of the tribe.

Bending over the dead deer, he drew out a hunting arrow and dropped it in his quiver.

"Now, War Cry, give your war cry!" whispered the boy.

The dog gave a single deep bark. Arrow Maker swung toward the river. As he saw the war canoe with its three gazing passengers, he stiffened with surprise. But he made no sound. Raising his hand with spread fingers, he turned it quickly from side to side. This was the question sign.

"He wants you to talk in sign language," whispered Dandelion. "Go on, answer him! I'll steer for you!" And he moved hastily into the stern of the boat.

Young Brave stood up. With one finger he drew a straight line across his forehead. Every Indian knew the meaning of this gesture. It meant *"Hat wearers,"* or, in other words, *"White men."*

"How many?" signaled the chief promptly, giving the question sign and then counting on his fingers.

Young Brave held up both hands, thumbs touching, fingers spread. Slowly he swung his hands in a big circle. This was the sign for one hundred. He made the circle twice, to show there were two hundred white men.

Arrow Maker looked at him calmly. Even better than the boy, he understood the terrible threat to his people. A lifetime of training kept him from showing what he felt. He only made the question sign again, then pointed in several directions. This meant *"Where?"*

Swiftly, the boy pointed across the river and downstream. Then he hesitated. He did not know any sign for ford. "Brother," he whispered, "how shall I tell him they are going to wade across at the ford?"

"Make the sign for river," whispered Dandelion. "Then make the sign for walk. River-walk — he will understand!"

"All right!" Young Brave raised his cupped hand to his mouth as if drinking. This was the water sign. Then he swept his hand sideways with a long, slow, wavy motion. Together with the water sign, this meant *"River."* Now he held out both hands, palms down. He made them seem to march forward like feet—*"Walk."* He paused, gazing anxiously at his father.

Did Arrow Maker understand? He turned, staring down the river. His keen profile showed no emotion, but there was something fierce in his intense gaze. Slowly he raised one clenched hand, then opened it with a sudden downward motion, as if throwing away something. This was the sign for *"Bad."* He swung back. His dark eyes met his son's.

"Bad!" agreed Young Brave, his heart thudding. Surely his message had been understood! There was one more thing he had to say. He held one hand high, like a tomahawk, brought it down hard on the palm of the other hand. This meant *"Attack!"*

A grim smile was the chief's answer. Then with

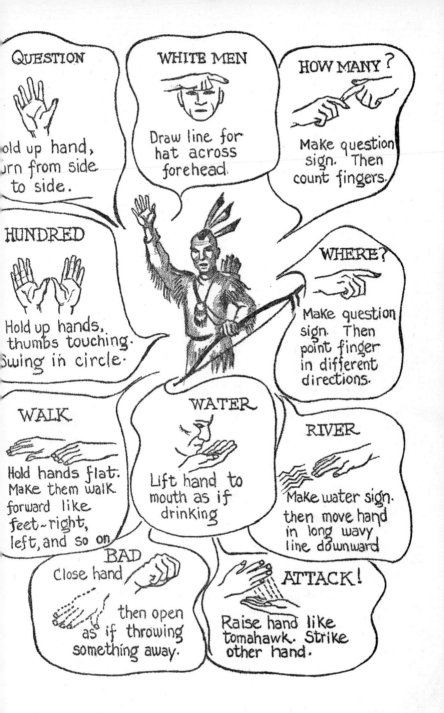

swift hand signs he signaled, *"Bring your canoe into the swamp and hide. Your part is finished. You have done well, both of you!"* He smiled again, this time with fond approval, glancing from boy to boy. The next instant he was gone, vanishing into the dark cedar as suddenly as an animal.

The swamp lay peaceful as before. But the cry of a hunting hawk rang out piercingly — twice, three times.

They looked at each other with shining eyes. "Father's signal," whispered Young Brave. "He's calling the warriors together."

"We've done it, we've done it! We carried the message!" crowed Dandelion. "And Keego said we'd fail!"

"Keego was wrong! Come on, let's land the canoe now!"

But Keego, after all, had been partly right. The war canoe, designed for men, was not easily to be controlled by two half-grown boys. Again and again they drove toward the western shore. Again and again the swift current whirled them back into the center of the river. The cedar swamp slipped by and was gone. Still they battled in silence, their thin bodies running with sweat. At last, almost at the same instant, they rested.

Dandelion laid his paddle across the bows. He fell forward across it, his shoulders heaving. "We can't make it, brother! We can't obey Arrow Maker! What are we going to do?"

Young Brave said, "We must keep on down the river to the ford!"

5
Wolf Man

DANDELION muttered something.

"What did you say?"

"I said we'd better not miss the ford!"

"Why not?"

"Because the Singing Water is just beyond."

A queer chill ran through Young Brave at the mention of the waterfall. But he answered steadily, "Of course we won't miss the ford! We'll wade ashore there, and hide in the forest. But we haven't much time. Don't forget, the white men are heading for the ford too, somewhere on the eastern bank."

"And so are the warriors, on the western bank!" Dandelion sat up, his blue eyes shining with excitement. "It's like a race, isn't it?"

"Yes," said the Indian boy grimly. "It's a race, and you and I must win it! Come on, let's paddle."

They resumed paddling. Now the river made a long swing to the east, and the current set in strongly toward the eastern shore. As they neared it, Young Brave looked hard at the sunny brown forest.

"Where can the white men be?" he muttered.

"I expect we've passed them," said Dandelion cheerfully. "Look out, there's driftwood ahead!"

Up at the next bend, a monster tree was wallowing along in the current. It was an oak uprooted by the flood. Brown leaves still clung and nodded on its great branches.

"It's hardly moving, it's so big," went on Dandelion. "If we're not careful, we're going to run right into it!"

But Young Brave was not listening. Somehow

he did not believe they had passed the enemy. And War Cry seemed to agree with him. The big dog was on his feet, staring at the eastern shore. What did his senses tell him? What danger lurked in that sunny forest?

And then Young Brave saw the red spot. It was moving down the wooded slope toward the bend, a spot of scarlet color. What could it be but the Captain's cloak?

He stopped paddling. Just as if he had been told, he knew now that the Captain had left his men on the trail and was coming down to the bend for a look up and down the river. Soon he would see the approaching canoe.

"What's the matter?" said Dandelion. "Why have you stopped paddling?" He turned around. How the sunlight glowed on his rosy face and blue eyes, his bright yellow hair! In spite of his deerskins, in spite of his feathered band, who could mistake him for an Indian?

Young Brave cried out hoarsely, "Get out of

sight — quick! Lie down in the bottom of the canoe!"

Dandelion had been trained to obey like an Indian boy. He flung himself down instantly. "What is it?" he whispered.

War Cry sprang past him into the bow. Placing his forefeet on the rail, he pointed his nose into the wind. A deep growl rumbled in his throat.

"We're passing the enemy. The white Captain is coming down to the water's edge. He mustn't see you!" said Young Brave.

"But he can see you!"

"What of that? Don't you understand? You're English!" cried Young Brave. "If they ever get a look at you, they'll try to rescue you! And they'll never give up!"

"Maybe I was English once, but I'm an Algonquin now," said Dandelion proudly. "I don't want to be rescued!"

"Then stay out of sight!"

"Yes, brother."

[63]

Young Brave paddled on, watching the bend. Nearer and nearer they came. He had lost sight of the red spot. Suddenly, right at the riverbank, the bushes parted. Helmet shining, red cloak swinging, the Captain stepped out into full view. He was not alone. A short, dark, broad-shouldered Indian emerged at his side. At once they saw the on-gliding canoe, the Indian boy, and the watchful dog. So near were they that Little Brave could see the Captain's start of surprise.

"They've seen me!" he whispered.

"They?"

"Wolf Man and the Captain."

Wolf Man's heavy face hardly changed expression, but his eyes narrowed to slits. Looking steadily at the boy, he drew a long, stone-tipped arrow from his quiver and fitted it to the string.

Young Brave felt very queer. A man was going to shoot at him, and he could not run away. But he could dodge! He could throw himself down! He went on paddling, his eyes on the arrow.

Slowly, Wolf Man raised his bow.

War Cry burst into frantic barking. Trained to the hunt, he understood perfectly what that arrow was meant to do.

"What's happening?" whispered Dandelion.

The Captain looked suddenly at his companion. With a startled exclamation, he knocked down the Indian's bow. The arrow dropped to the ground.

Wolf Man whirled and faced him. His words came clearly over the water: "Why did you knock down my bow? The boy has seen you! Unless I kill him, he'll give the alarm!"

"Put away your arrow!" answered the Captain, in the Algonquin language.

"Why?"

"Because I will not let you shoot a child!"

"All white men are not so kindhearted," said the renegade, with a sneer. "And you, of all men, shouldn't feel sorry for an Indian boy. Have you forgotten that your own child was killed by Indians?"

"Put away your arrow!" The Captain had not raised his voice, but there was something in his tone which made the Indian jump. Without another word he snatched up his arrow and dropped it into the quiver. Then he turned a dark and venomous look on the boy in the canoe.

Young Brave shivered. What had Keego said?

When Wolf Man was angry, the children used to hide! But now he could not hide.

The dog had stopped barking. His yellow eyes remained fixed on the renegade, and his white teeth showed in a savage, silent snarl.

"Brother," whispered Dandelion, "you know I can't see what's happening. Tell me, or I'll stand up!"

"Wolf Man just tried to shoot me, but the Captain stopped him. Now he's very angry. I think he'll try again!"

"Won't you lie down in the bottom of the canoe?"

"Then who would steer? Don't worry," said Young Brave coolly. "I've got my eye on him! Anyhow, we'll soon be out of range. We're passing them right now. As for the alarm, it's already been given. Wolf Man is too late, though he doesn't know it!" And he laughed aloud.

Almost at once he regretted that laugh, for as the light sound of it floated over the water, Wolf

[67]

Man's eyes seemed to flame with rage. Leaping back from the Captain, he drew an arrow from his quiver and fitted it to the string in an instant. But the white man was as quick as he. Wheeling, he caught the Indian's arm just as the arrow left the string.

"A miss!" thought Young Brave, as he flung himself down.

Thud!

With a yelp, War Cry went hurtling from the canoe and fell with a heavy splash into the river.

"He's killed our dog, the coward!" screamed Dandelion.

There was a long grating sound, followed by the crack of ripping birchbark. The canoe slowed and stopped. Great branches appeared all around it, their brown leaves waving and rustling. The spike of a broken branch pierced the bow.

They had run into the floating oak tree.

6

Trouble

FOR A MOMENT, Young Brave lay with closed eyes. Or was it longer than a moment? He felt overwhelmed. Too many bad things had happened too fast. His beloved dog was gone. His canoe was wrecked. What would his enemies do to him now that he was helpless? But he must watch them! He got to his feet, peering cautiously through the brown leaves that hung all around him.

The Captain was holding Wolf Man's bow. "The boy's canoe is stuck fast," he was saying. "He certainly can't give the alarm now! Will you come along?"

"Give me my bow," muttered Wolf Man.

"Here it is. You and I will have a talk later. I don't like tricks! Now we must catch up with the men. Hurry! No, you first!"

Wolf Man slunk into the forest, and the Captain followed.

"Brother," whispered Young Brave, "they've gone away." There was no answer. Turning, he found that he was alone in the canoe.

Dandelion was gone!

Cold fear seized him. Had that whizzing arrow struck Dandelion instead of War Cry? But he himself had seen the dog's brown body hurtling from the canoe! Then where was his English brother? Wildly he gazed around, but saw only the trembling oak leaves, the flashing water. Caught in the upper branches of the great tree, the war canoe moved slowly, slowly onward with its single passenger. Was this a bad dream? *"Dandelion!"* he cried out in despair. And wonder of wonders, a voice answered, a familiar voice, from nearby.

"Here I am!"

"Where?"

"Underneath these leaves! Don't you see me?" And a thin arm shot up through the mass of leaves on the west side of the canoe and waved wildly. "Hurry up and help me! I can't make it!"

"Are you hurt?"

"No!"

"Then what's the matter?"

"You think I can swim through a tree with a dog in my arms?" sputtered Dandelion.

Young Brave cried joyfully, "You've got the dog!"

"Of course! That's why I jumped overboard. But he's hurt. Give me a hand, won't you?"

"Here, catch hold of my paddle!" Young Brave held out the paddle, and Dandelion grasped the tip with one hand while with the other he carefully held the dog's head above water. Slowly, Young Brave drew them toward the canoe.

"Now take the dog!" gasped Dandelion.

"Got him!"

"All right. I'll balance the canoe while you pull him in." Diving under the canoe, Dandelion came up on the other side, gripped the rail and hung there. "Pull away!"

Young Brave pulled, his arms locked around the body of his dog friend. How heavy it was, that wet, limp body! Up, up it came, up and over the canoe rim and down into the bottom of the boat. He sat back, wiping the sweat from his eyes. Was it sweat? Or tears?

The big dog lay on his side, limp and still. His eyes were shut; his red tongue lolled from the corner of his mouth. Water streamed from his shaggy coat.

Young Brave stared at the dog silently. He was only a boy. All he could do was to grieve, and because he was an Indian boy, he must hide his grief. But if he were a warrior, what things he would do to Wolf Man for this deed! He would take up his trail — he would follow him night and day — he would never rest until he had avenged his beloved dog.

"I saw him fall overboard. He wasn't swimming, so I dove after him," explained Dandelion, climbing into the canoe. "Why would they shoot a poor dog?"

"It was Wolf Man! He was aiming at me. The Captain grabbed him, and the arrow went wild. War Cry died in my place!" said Young Brave.

"Died? Is he dead? Are you sure?"

"Well, look at him! The arrow isn't sticking in him, is it? So it must have gone clean through him. We're hunters! We know what an arrow does to an animal. Either he's dead, or soon will be."

"But he can't die! I won't let him!" cried Dandelion, fiercely dashing away his tears. "I'll find the wound and bandage it! I'll save him!" On his knees, and sobbing in spite of himself, he began examining the still body of the dog.

The Indian boy did not watch. Bitterly he fixed his eyes on that part of the forest where Wolf Man had disappeared. Vengeful dreams passed through his mind. He was roused by a loud cry from Dandelion.

"He isn't wounded!"

"What?"

"See for yourself!"

"Not wounded?" Then Young Brave too examined the dog. He looked up, bewildered. "You're right, there's not a mark on him. But I know he was hit!"

"So do I!" cried Dandelion. "I heard the thud!"

"And I saw the arrow! Where is that arrow? *What kind of arrow was it?*" Young Brave stood up. A tuft of white, fixed in the leafy oak branches ahead, caught his eye. He ran forward. Leaning out over the bow of the canoe, he plucked something from the branches. Silently he held it up for Dandelion to see.

It was a long arrow, tufted at one end with white feathers. The other end was peculiar. Instead of the cruel stone tip used in war, this arrow bore only a big, blunt wooden knob.

"Why — why, it's a bird bolt!" gasped Dandelion. "Wolf Man shot our dog with a bird bolt!"

They burst into shouts of laughter.

"The joke's on him!" chuckled Young Brave. "He pulled out a bird bolt instead of a war arrow and never noticed, because he was in such a rage. Why, a bird bolt can only knock down small game. Our dog isn't dead!"

"He can't be!" cried Dandelion. "That bird bolt just bounced off his head and into the oak tree! He's only stunned. Look, look!"

War Cry had raised his head. Perhaps by now the effects of the blow had worn off, or perhaps he had been roused by the laughter of the boys. His yellow eyes, dazed but loving, looked from one young face to the other, while his tail beat out a joyous message on the floor of the canoe — *thump, thump!*

With a glad cry, Dandelion flung himself on the dog. Young Brave said softly, "This is your doing, brother! He would have drowned if you hadn't been so quick to help him."

"Never mind that!"

"But you took a great risk. The white man might have seen you."

"No such thing! Don't forget, we ran into the

oak tree just then. The branches were all around. He couldn't have seen me!"

"Well, be careful! If they ever see you, we'll be in trouble."

"Talking of trouble," said Dandelion, "how are we going to get free of this oak?"

Both boys now turned their attention to the canoe. It was a helpless captive. Hooked on the broken branch, and held in the snare of the surrounding leafy mass, it could move only at the pace of the tree. And what a sluggish pace that was!

Young Brave muttered, "Why, we haven't even passed the bend!"

Before this accident, they had had a good chance of winning the race to the ford. But now? Precious minutes had been lost during their fright and grief about War Cry. Even if they got free, could they overtake the enemy? They must try, at any rate!

Together they hurried to the broken branch that

stuck through the birchbark into the bow. Luckily, the rip was above the waterline. If they could only push the branch out, they would be free. They pushed and shoved, but the current, acting from behind, only drove them farther onto the oak.

Unexpectedly, the tree itself came to their rescue. As it moved around the bend, it turned. The heavy root end swung toward the eastern shore. The upper branches, with the canoe, swung out into the channel. Here the current tugged at the canoe with eager force. The mass of the tree lay off to one side. Clear water lay ahead.

Young Brave stood in the stern, paddling hard. Dandelion, crouching in the bow, shoved with all his might on the oak branch. It yielded, it was gone. The freed canoe slipped away downstream at its own arrowy pace. Both boys yelled with triumph.

"We're off!" shouted Young Brave.

Again they seized their paddles. The drowned shores slipped by as before. Minutes passed. They saw neither white man nor red man. As they approached the last bend, Young Brave listened hard for sounds of battle. But he heard only the rush of the river, the clear whistling of birds, the distant mutter of the Singing Water.

"Are we in time, after all?" he thought. But he said nothing. Dandelion too was tense and silent.

The dog, feeling their suspense, staggered to his feet. As silent as his masters, he gazed forward with unwinking yellow eyes.

Around the last bend they whirled. And now the ford lay open before them, a long stretch of rocky shallow. Beyond it the river ran on past All Alone Rock and down to the Singing Water.

Young Brave stiffened. He heard Dandelion's gasp of dismay, War Cry's deep growl. He said quietly, "We're too late!"

The English war party had reached the ford. Two by two, they were marching down from the forest, plunging waist-deep into the river, and wading sturdily across, muskets and powder horns held high. The Captain and Wolf Man led them. Already they had passed the middle point.

The race to the ford was won and lost. And the enemy had won it.

7

The Fight
at the Ford

"WHERE are my father's warriors?" Despairingly, Young Brave scanned the western shore. Here the pine forest sprang thick and green from the water's edge. Floodwater had run back among the trees. It gleamed and rippled, but nothing else moved there. No Indian arrow flew.

"Do you see them?" whispered Dandelion. He had crouched down quickly in the bow, hiding himself from the white men. Pale with shock, he was watching his brother's face.

"No," answered Young Brave calmly. "They

are not here. Something has gone wrong. Maybe we brought our message too late. Maybe Arrow Maker didn't understand."

"We did our best!"

"Yes, we did our best!"

"Will we be captured?"

"Of course. They won't hurt you, because you are English. But me —"

Already the approaching canoe had been noticed. Bearded white faces were turning, scowling at the Algonquin boy. No indeed, all white men were not merciful like the Captain!

Dandelion whispered, "I won't let them hurt you!"

Young Brave was silent. He felt no fear, only a great awe. What did his own danger matter when all his people were doomed? And doomed they surely were. Only here at the ford could the enemy be stopped, and no one was stopping them. Soon they would be marching on the helpless village. By tomorrow morning, this little tribe of the great

Algonquin nation would have vanished forever from the pleasant forest.

A terrible sound split the air. It was like the scream of the cougar, the shriek of the wolverine, the howl of the storm wind. But it was none of these. It was the Algonquin war whoop. A cloud of arrows flew from the pine forest on the western shore, that very shore that had seemed so deserted. Shouts, cries broke from the white men.

Fierce joy thrilled the Indian boy. Shaking his paddle aloft like a tomahawk, he joined loudly in the war whoop. Dandelion yelled with him, and the dog bayed in his deep voice. Not for nothing was he named War Cry!

"Arrow Maker is here!" shouted Young Brave. "He understood us, he brought his warriors! It's an ambush!"

The Algonquins had planned well. Hidden in the forest, they had allowed the unsuspecting enemy to advance toward them across the river. Now, when the range was best, they had launched their arrows.

"Our village is saved!" cried Dandelion, peeping recklessly over the bow. "Look, look at the enemy!"

"Keep out of sight, brother!"

"Do you think they have time for me?"

Panic had seized the English war party. They were not regular troops, only farmers and traders on an expedition intended to punish the Indians for their raids. Exposed to the fire of unseen foemen, and taken by surprise, they fell into wild confusion. Their orderly double file broke up. Some men turned back, some stood still, some advanced. Some had fallen, and some were clutching at fallen comrades.

The Captain turned, bellowing orders for retreat.

"They're turning back!" shouted Young Brave.

Still under a rain of arrows, the men in the water struggled toward the shore. Those still on the shore dashed back into the forest.

Dandelion burst into a laugh. "Look at Wolf Man go! He ought to be called Fish Man, he's so fast in the water!"

Young Brave said grimly, "He'd better hurry!"

At the first sound of the war whoop, the renegade had turned to flee. Terror gave him speed, and already he had nearly reached the shore. But sharp eyes had seen him, and many a good bowman was aiming at him. Suddenly he threw up his hands and fell forward, an arrow in his back. The river whirled him on, on toward the Singing Water.

One by one the white men were gaining the bank. Last of all came the Captain, wading steadily, his arm around a wounded man. Through the war whoops, he could be heard shouting encouragement to his men. Arrows splashed all around him, but he did not turn his head.

"I hope he won't get hit," muttered Young Brave.

"Who?"

"The Captain."

Dandelion's eyes shone. "Oh yes! He protected you from Wolf Man. Look how calm he is! I hope he'll reach the bank safely."

And the Captain did. Still without haste, he directed the wounded man back into the forest. Then he himself stepped behind a stout cedar tree on the riverbank and loaded his musket. As he leaned out to fire, sunlight flashed again from his steel helmet.

Young Brave grunted. Surely the man knew what a mark he was! Why didn't he take off that shiny helmet?

Meanwhile, the war canoe was nearing the ford. The white men had all taken cover by now, but they had not quit. Puffs of smoke burst from the forest. Balls tore across the river. The crash of muskets echoed and re-echoed from the hills around. The Algonquins replied with whizzing arrows. And down into this cross-fire swept the war canoe, with its three helpless passengers.

Neither boy noticed the danger. They were busy watching the show. Only the dog, unused to the sound of gunfire, felt afraid. Trembling, he crept close to Young Brave.

Sssssssss! Something passed over the canoe, between the two boys.

"What was that?" cried Dandelion.

[87]

Young Brave paused, then went on paddling. "That was an arrow!"

"Algonquins, hold your fire! My sons are in that canoe!" Chief Arrow Maker's voice rang with deadly fear.

The yells of the Indians died away. No more arrows flew from the western shore. On the east, the musket fire kept up with unabated fury. Balls whistled around the canoe.

"Brother," cried Dandelion, "aren't we over the ford yet? Can't we jump out and make a run for it?"

"No," answered Young Brave. "The water is still deep here. I must steer, and you must lie flat. Please, brother! Lie flat!"

"I won't," muttered Dandelion. "Not while you're making a target of yourself!" And he continued to peep over the side. Presently he gave a glad cry. "It's all right! They won't fire any more! The Captain is telling them to stop!"

The white leader was pointing at the canoe

and shouting orders. It was plain that he meant his men to cease firing. But the farmer-soldiers were too angry to listen. Only for a moment the firing slacked off. Then it began again with new fury. There were Indians to shoot at across the river, and for that matter, there was an Indian in the canoe. *Crack, crack!*

"He told them to stop, and they're still firing!" cried Dandelion.

Young Brave said quietly, "Even a chief can't always control his men."

"But some of them are firing at *you!*"

"Why not? After all, I'm their enemy!"

To Young Brave, it did not seem strange that war should be made on children. He knew that Indians seldom spared the children of their enemies. But Dandelion, long ago, had had a different training. Red with surprise and anger, he stared at those disobedient soldiers who were shooting at his friend.

There was a whining sound as a musket ball

passed directly over Young Brave's head. Putting up his hand, he found that his hawk feather had been cut clean off. He shuddered in spite of himself.

"What's the matter?" cried Dandelion.

"Nothing," muttered Young Brave. "A ball went over my head."

"And clipped the feather!"

"Yes, it clipped the feather."

"As close as that!"

"Never mind, brother! Don't do it, don't do it!"

But the English boy had leaped to his feet. Straight and fair he stood in the brilliant autumn sunshine, his blue eyes blazing in his flushed face. "You cowards!" he shouted. "You nearly killed my brother! Do you call yourselves warriors? Why don't you obey your chief? Oh, if I could still speak your language, I'd make you listen to me!"

Young Brave groaned aloud. Dandelion did not need the English language to make the white men listen!

All along the eastern shore, amazed faces peered at the yellow-haired boy in the canoe. The firing died away. The echoes died away.

The silence that followed was broken in a strange way.

Dropping his musket with a crash, the Captain sprang out from behind the cedar tree. *"Jonathan!"* he cried.

[91]

8

All Alone Rock

DANDELION made no response. All color drained from his face, and he looked stunned.

"Jonathan!" cried the Captain again.

A memory stirred in Young Brave's mind. Long ago, when Dandelion was first captured, he used to repeat his name, a strange English name that an Indian boy could hardly pronounce. Was this the name? If so, who was this white man?

Young Brave looked from yellow-haired boy to

yellow-bearded man. Suddenly an idea came to him. It was a bitter idea, and he ground his teeth with the pain of it. Of course Dandelion must have a father somewhere — and not very far away! He had been captured in a nearby town. But who would have dreamed that that father would ever appear? Had he appeared now? Wolf Man had said that the Captain's child had been killed by Indians. Was there some mistake about that? Had the child lived? Was Dandelion that child? The Captain seemed to think so! What about Dandelion? Did he guess?

They were over the ford now. Gray ledges lay beneath the water, but Young Brave did not notice. He was watching the Captain, who was running along the bank in an effort to keep up with the canoe. Strangely enough, no one shot at him. Indians and white men watched in amazed silence. As he ran, he shouted questions in English.

"Is he calling to me?" whispered Dandelion. "Brother, who is he?"

Young Brave almost laughed, so great was his relief. Dandelion was still in the dark, and he, Young Brave, would certainly not enlighten him. He would keep his adopted brother, Captain or no Captain! "Don't you know?" he said lightly. "That's the enemy chief!"

"Yes, yes," whispered Dandelion, *"but who is he?"*

A warning cry rang out from the western shore. Chief Arrow Maker too had stepped from cover. Painted for war, there he stood on the riverbank. He was a clear target, yet no white man fired.

"My sons, you're passing the ford!" he cried harshly. "Leave the canoe now! Quick, quick, before it's too late!"

All at once, Young Brave became aware of a strange sound all about him. How could he have been deaf to it before? It filled the air. It shook the frame of the canoe. It was the voice of the Singing Water. But the waterfall was not singing today. It was roaring, with a deep and dangerous note like the Thunderbird calling in the storm clouds.

He threw down his paddle. "Brother, come on! We've got to get ashore!"

"Wait!"

"But we can't wait!"

"I said wait!" Dandelion was himself again. Seizing a paddle, he thrust it down, down into the water. Withdrawing it, he looked calmly at Young Brave. "The water is up to our eyes! We can't make it! We should be swept away!"

"But this is the ford!"

"It's the ford in floodtime!"

Helplessly, Young Brave turned to his father. He held out both hands. "How can we obey you? The water is too deep for us!"

With a hoarse cry, Arrow Maker plunged into the river and waded toward them. From the other bank, the Captain too rushed out on the ford. But the swift current was whirling the canoe onward. The gray ledges dropped away, the water deepened. They had passed the ford, and now they were on their way to the Singing Water.

Downstream, beyond the black bulk of All Alone Rock, the river shone with a dazzling brightness. Smooth and swift and straight it ran, on toward the waterfall.

Young Brave looked back. He saw that the two men had met on the ford. Side by side they stood, gazing after the children. Bearded white face and painted dark face wore the same look of horror.

"So I was right!" he thought. "The Captain *is* Dandelion's father! He must be, because he's as scared as my father!"

Just then the two men glanced at each other. Some unspoken thought seemed to pass between them. Separating, each waded hastily toward his own shore. And still no arrow flew, no musket fired.

"Well?" said Dandelion. Serene and bright-eyed, very alert, he was wearing his "danger face" again. Unexpected fathers he might not know how to deal with, but a river was something he understood.

[97]

Young Brave smiled at him. "We still have a chance!"

"Yes," said Dandelion.

"All Alone Rock!" said Young Brave.

"All Alone Rock," agreed Dandelion.

"Let's paddle!"

They dipped their paddles like one boy.

All Alone Rock was an island. A single great black rock, it stood alone at the edge of the channel half a mile above the waterfall. It was near the eastern shore.

There was a game about All Alone Rock. Young Brave remembered it now. It was a dangerous game, a real test of courage. Only the older Indian boys played it. Daring each other, they would launch their canoes in the swift current at the ford. Then they would try to reach the rock. If they could touch there, seize the rock, and stop their canoes, they were safe. From the eastern side they could paddle through calmer water to the nearby shore. If they missed, they went over the falls.

Young Brave had never seen a boy miss — except on that one day which had given him his secret fear of the Singing Water. Now he must face its dangers, yet the old fear seemed to have left him. He felt calm and strong. "Manitou is still with me!" he told himself. Paddling as he had never paddled before, with long sure strokes he drove the canoe toward All Alone Rock. Up in the bow, Dandelion too was paddling with new vigor. The current helped, sweeping them rapidly toward the great rock.

Arrow Maker and the Captain were running along opposite banks of the river, keeping up with the canoe. As they ran, they called out to each other like friends. Young Brave listened wonderingly. He heard the Captain shout in Algonquin, "They'll make it!" And Arrow Maker shouted back, "One of them will make it!" What did he mean? The shout seemed to echo and re-echo in the boy's mind. "One of them will make it!" Glancing again at the shore, he saw that his father had stopped running and was staring at him with a fixed and terrible look. The Captain still ran on, but now he was holding up his clasped hands. Was he praying as he ran? What was the matter? What did the men know that he had not guessed?

"Keep her as she is!" Dandelion was shouting joyously. "We'll strike bow on!"

"And you will jump out," thought Young Brave. "And I?" Suddenly he understood. There would be no stopping at All Alone Rock today — not in this flood! They could only touch, touch for an instant. And if the boy in the bow leaped out, what would happen to the other boy? Would he too be able to make his jump, or, losing control of the canoe, would he be swept helplessly on, on over the falls?

Just for a second, his old fear returned. His

stroke faltered, and the canoe wavered in its course.

Dandelion looked round at once, anxiety flashing in his blue eyes. "Are you all right, brother? Keep paddling — we're nearly there!"

Young Brave shook himself. This was no time to give up! After all, there were two boys in the canoe! And the other was Dandelion.

For six winters and six summers they had been friends and brothers. They had told no lies to each other, kept no secrets from each other. They had shared everything, even their dog. They had trusted each other, and neither had failed that trust.

Young Brave would not fail it now. Whatever followed, he would do his best for his brother.

Paddling furiously, he shouted: "Get ready to jump!"

"I'm ready! What about War Cry?"

The big dog was crouching in the bottom of the canoe. Terrified by the roar of the falls, he had crept close to Young Brave and was watching him with shining yellow eyes. Here was another who trusted the Indian boy!

"Call him into the bow! He must jump with you!"

"Come here, War Cry!"

But for the first time in his life War Cry disobeyed. He did not move.

All Alone Rock loomed before them, black and huge, steep-sided, flat-topped. Bow on, they plunged toward it.

"Now!" shouted Young Brave.

They struck. Standing up and throwing away his paddle, Dandelion jumped. His fingers caught the top of the rock. He dangled, he pulled himself up over the edge and onto the flat summit. He was safe.

And Young Brave? He too was ready to jump. Oh yes, he was ready! But there was no chance for him. Just as he had foreseen, his friend's leap threw the recoiling canoe sharply away from the rock. Raging water lay between him and safety. It widened, widened. Savagely he drove his paddle. What was the use? How could he control the canoe, alone, against such a current?

He was passing All Alone Rock. He had passed it.

He stopped paddling.

9

The
Singing Water

MEN shouted. The waterfall roared. But above all other sounds rang a despairing scream: "Come back, come back!"

Dandelion was standing motionless on the top of All Alone Rock. Already he seemed far away, like a boy seen in a dream. Very vivid he was, against the fair blue sky, a slim, yellow-haired boy in brown deerskins mottled with dark wet patches. His face was blanched, his eyes stared. He did not scream again.

Young Brave raised his paddle in farewell.

Then he tossed it over the side. "My brother is safe! You could have been safe too, War Cry! But you chose to stay with me. Thank you for that! Now you must be very brave. Stand up! Come here!"

Obediently, the dog staggered to his feet. That watery roaring was growing louder. Instinct told him he was in deadly danger, but his master had spoken. He took his place beside the boy.

Young Brave stood very straight, his hand on the dog's head. Pride surged up in him, Indian pride, one of the strongest feelings known to man or boy. "We are Indians, you and I! Enemies are watching. We will show them whether Indians are afraid!"

Swiftly, the dog licked his hand. Then he stared ahead, his yellow eyes steady.

Boy and dog waited. The canoe shook with its speed, but did not rock, for the river was strangely smooth as it rushed to the falls. It was easy to keep balance.

Arrow Maker was plunging through the dense and tangled forest on the west.

"He is going to the whirlpool below the falls! But there's no trail on that side. He'll be late, much too late!"

Flash after flash of brightness showed that the helmeted Captain was bounding down the rocks on the east.

"There's a portage trail there, but he is an enemy! Why is he going to the whirlpool?"

Back at the ford, Indian warriors and white soldiers lined the riverbanks. All were watching him in silent horror.

"At least the battle is over. Will they fight any more? Perhaps I have done something for my people! What do you think, War Cry? Will they remember you and me?"

The Singing Water was very close now. The brim shone white as lightning. Clouds of mist drifted up from below. The noise was deafening.

Young Brave shut his eyes, then opened them

resolutely. He gazed straight ahead into the mist cloud. Under his hand the dog stood motionless.

"Here we go!"

He flung himself on the dog.

The bow shot out over nothingness, then pointed horribly down. As they dropped, Young Brave had an instant of wonder at the skill with which the great war canoe, seemingly alive, glided down the long cataract. It struck hard, then dove under a great dome of water with the alert ease of a fish.

Water overwhelmed him, boiled over him, flung him this way and that. The canoe was gone. Would they never come up? He was suffocating. The dog struggled wildly in his arms. There was a roaring in his ears, fiery darkness before his eyes.

The grip of the whirlpool slackened. His head shot out of water. He saw blue sky, a foam-flecked pool, whirling mists. He gulped air, swallowed water. He could not touch bottom. It was too late. The dog was heavy. As for himself, he no longer

cared. His eyes closed. Water ran into his open mouth.

A hand seized him. A strong arm passed around him. "It is Father," thought Young Brave. "He will never be able to save us. We are too heavy!" But he clung stubbornly to his dog.

His head lay on someone's broad chest. Someone was swimming, towing boy and dog.

They reached shallow water. Someone stood up, lifted boy and dog together, and holding them in his great arms, waded ashore. Someone placed them side by side on the bank, knelt down, and raised Young Brave's head with a gentle hand.

"Father!" murmured the boy. A dreamy happiness filled him. He had gone over the falls and under the whirlpool, and lived; he had brought his dog with him. He had shown no fear. Now the ordeal was over, and he was safe at last with Arrow Maker. Smiling, he opened his eyes.

He looked straight into the face of the Captain.

10

Captured!

GASPING with terror, Young Brave tried to sit up. But he was too weak. He fell back, sick and dizzy, his eyes on the face above him.

Never before had he been close to a white man! The high, narrow helmet shone with a terrible light; the golden beard seemed strange and dreadful. Indian men had no hair on their faces. But the blue eyes looked very friendly, and now the Captain smiled.

"Don't be afraid of me," he said in Algonquin. "I won't hurt you!"

War Cry stirred at the sound of the strange voice. A growl rumbled in his throat.

"Don't growl at him!" whispered Young Brave. "He's a friend — though I don't know why!" He looked up at the white man. "You pulled us out of the water when we were drowning. Thank you! But I don't understand. Why did you do it?"

"Because —" The Captain groped for words. He was not smiling now, but his eyes looked kinder than ever. "Because I saw you put that other boy ashore on the big rock! That was brave! After that, could I let you drown?"

Young Brave swallowed. "You know that other boy?"

The Captain said simply, "I think I know him. But I'm not sure. Can you help me? Who is he?"

"His name is Dandelion. He's my brother."

"But he is white!"

"Yes, of course. He's my white brother."

"When did he come to live with you?"

But Young Brave would not answer any more

questions. The Captain wanted to take his brother away, that was clear! He lay silent.

Through the thunder of the falls rang a harsh cry. "Englishman! Is my son alive?"

Chief Arrow Maker stood on the far side of the whirlpool, his chest heaving, his deerskins torn by his wild race through the forest. Clouds of mist blew past him.

Young Brave cried out joyfully, "I'm all right, Father, and so is War Cry! The Captain saved us!"

Arrow Maker bowed his head. He stood quite still, seeming to ponder. The mist clouds whirled and drifted. At last he looked up, his painted face marked with the lines of inner struggle. "The Captain has done me a great service! I must repay him, and I will!" Turning, he ran into the forest.

"Father!" cried Young Brave.

But Arrow Maker was gone.

The boy rolled over, burying his face in his

arms. Why had his father gone away and left him with the white man? What would become of him now?

How cold the wind was! All at once he knew that he was chilled and exhausted, that his wet deerskins clung unpleasantly, that for a long time he hadn't had enough to eat. He began to shiver like a sick person. War Cry, getting up, nuzzled anxiously at his face and whimpered. But Young Brave paid no attention.

Something thick and soft and warm fell over him. The Captain was lifting him, wrapping him in the folds of the scarlet cloak, which he had taken off before plunging into the water. What was it made of, that wonderful cloak? Of course it was made of wool, but Young Brave had never heard of wool. He knew only that no deerskin ever felt so comforting as that unknown fabric. And now the Captain picked him up bodily.

"Come, my boy! Let's go meet the others. Some-one is waiting for you."

[114]

"Oh," murmured Young Brave. "You mean Dandelion!"

The Captain smiled. "Yes, I mean Dandelion. He thinks you are drowned, you know!"

In spite of himself, Young Brave smiled back. "That's true! Won't he be glad to see me!"

"Of course he will! Call your dog."

"Come, War Cry!"

And so they set off, the Captain carrying the boy, and the dog following. Up the steep portage trail they went, alongside the Singing Water, back towards All Alone Rock and the ford.

It seemed a long way. Young Brave grew more and more excited. He kept remembering Dandelion as he had last seen him, standing on All Alone Rock against the blue sky. Was he still there? But perhaps he had tried to swim ashore. In ordinary times that could be done, but not in floodtime. Why hadn't Young Brave warned him?

How slowly the Captain was climbing! Couldn't those long legs of his move a little faster?

As they approached the top, the Captain began shouting in English. Voices answered. White men came running to meet them. They crowded around the Captain, talking excitedly in English, and staring at the Algonquin boy. Their faces were kind, but Young Brave tingled with impatience. The Captain had halted. Here they were at the top of the trail, and he could not see the river. Those English faces were blocking his view!

He began to struggle. With a laugh, the Captain set him down. Shaking off the cloak, he darted through the ring of men and faced the river.

For a moment the sunlit water blinded him. Then, as his sight cleared, he saw All Alone Rock. There it stood as before, a dark island in the dazzling water. But there was one change. No yellow-haired boy was standing on its grim summit, outlined against the blue sky.

Dandelion was gone!

Young Brave had already borne a great deal that day. This last shock was too much. He let out his breath with a whistling sound. His legs gave way. As he sank to the ground, the Captain ran up and caught him.

"Here, here, my boy! What's the matter?"

"He's gone!"

"Who's gone?"

"My brother!"

"Oh, so that's it!" To Young Brave's bewilderment, the Captain gave a quiet chuckle. Then he lifted the boy in his arms, swung him up, and seated him firmly on his shoulder. "Take another look," he advised.

Young Brave obeyed. His dizziness passed away. Again the river flashed, again the rock rose grim and solitary. But this time, from his high perch, he made out what he had missed before — a brown-clad boy lying face down on the level summit.

He gave a jump of joy that nearly unseated him. "It's Dandelion!" he cried. "He's still there! But what is he doing?"

"Grieving for his red brother," said the Captain gently. "Better call to him."

Promptly, Young Brave cupped his hands around his mouth. There was a private signal cry that he always used when he lost Dandelion in the forest. It was the cry of the dog-fox, a high-pitched, yelping snarl. Now he sent it ringing across the water. *"Yap yurr! Yap yurr!"*

Up sprang Dandelion. Amazed, he stared at

the group on the riverbank. Who was that, seated on the Captain's shoulder and waving at him frantically? Could it be Young Brave, who had placed him on All Alone Rock and then ridden so boldly in the war canoe over the brim of the Singing Water? And that big tawny dog, panting and grinning, could it be the lost War Cry? Yes, yes! Wonder of wonders, his friends had survived the terrible plunge. Shrilly he greeted them with the proper answer, the cry of the she-fox: *"Yap yurr! Yurr yeow!"*

He began to dance. And Young Brave, slipping from the Captain's shoulder, danced too. White men looked on smilingly as the two friends danced out their great joy, one on the rock and one on the shore.

"Whew!" gasped Young Brave. Exhausted, he checked his dance and sat down. All at once he noticed the onlookers. They had all come up now, the whole great company of farmer-soldiers. What a crowd! His whole tribe, women and children and all, would not have numbered so many. He felt overwhelmed.

War Cry trotted up, and he threw his arms around the dog's sturdy neck. "We're captives," he whispered. "What will become of us?"

But War Cry could not tell him.

On the opposite bank, not a single Algonquin warrior was to be seen. Where were his friends? Above all, where was his father?

Dandelion too checked his dance. Just as Young Brave had done, he seemed all at once to realize his plight. He called out loudly, "Brother, how can I escape from this rock? How can I get to you?"

"Don't try!" answered the Indian boy. "Can't you see I'm a captive?"

"Then I want to be a captive too! Shall I swim?"

"Stay where you are! The river is too dangerous!"

Dandelion hesitated. Then he too sat down.

Hugging his knees, he gazed sorrowfully at the raging water.

The Captain was in earnest talk with the other officers. The rest of the company were taking their ease. Some were cleaning their muskets, others were opening food pouches. Several men offered him food, but he refused courteously. Hungry as he was, just then he could not have swallowed a morsel. There was a lump in his throat, a sore feeling in his chest. "If I were a little girl like Cricket," he thought, "I would cry!" But he did not cry.

What would the Englishmen do with him? Would they take him to their town beyond the hills? There, he had heard, they lived in great strong wigwams of stone and wood. Unlike Indians, they spent much of their time indoors. They seldom hunted. They never spent long joyous days in the forest, learning the secrets of the animals.

Animals, so Young Brave had been taught, had their tribes just like men. There were the

Beaver Tribe, the Deer Tribe, the Muskrat Tribe, and so on. Each had its own gifts, tricks, powers, and customs. Some even had their own land, which they defended like warriors.

But the white men did not care about such things. When they went out under the blue sky, they only dug or planted their fields, work that in Indian villages was left to women. How could an Indian boy bear such a life?

Once his grandfather, wise old Cloud Man, had said to him: "White men's ways are good for white men. Indian ways are good for Indians. Each must be true to his own!"

Surely his grandfather was right. He, Young Brave, must be true to Indian ways.

Then what of Dandelion? Did the English boy, too, need to grow up according to the ways of his own people? Perhaps the Indians were wrong to keep him here in the forest, a white captive, learning the ways of Indians. Should they let him go?

[122]

"But I don't want to let my brother go!" thought Young Brave.

He sighed heavily. How tired he was! He was stretched out now, his head resting comfortably on the shaggy body of War Cry, who was fast asleep. Someone had spread a cloak over him, that same thick scarlet cloak. Worn out in mind and body, he fell into a sudden deep sleep.

Excited shouts waked him.

11

Who Is Dandelion?

INDIAN BOYS were trained to wake fast. So were Indian dogs. Young Brave and War Cry were on their feet in an instant.

A white soldier stood on the riverbank, shouting excitedly. He was pointing upstream.

Young Brave looked that way. He caught his breath, and his dark eyes flashed with emotion.

"War Cry," he whispered, "look!"

A canoe had rounded the bend. It was small and light, a neat birchbark craft with a dark wolftail flying from the stern. A single Indian knelt in it, driving it onward with swift hard strokes.

It was Arrow Maker, chief of the Blue River Indians.

"He didn't forget us, War Cry! I knew he wouldn't! After he left us, he must have gone back to the cedar swamp for his boat. But what is he going to do? He's alone. Will they shoot at him?"

Amazed and curious, most of the soldiers were crowding forward to watch the approaching canoe. A few were readying their muskets for fire.

The Captain strode up to him. "My boy, what is this? Does your father come as a friend?"

"I don't know!"

"He is unarmed," muttered the Captain. Turning to his men, he shouted an order. All muskets were put down.

Arrow Maker reached the ford. But he did not stop there. Paddling rapidly over the shallows, he drove the canoe forward into deep water. The swift current seized it, carrying it toward All Alone Rock and the Singing Water.

Wondering cries broke from the white men. The Captain seized Young Brave's arm. "Look, look, he's going to try for a rescue! Can he make it?"

Young Brave wrenched away. "Yes, he'll make it!" And he raised his war whoop. "On to All Alone Rock! On, on, Arrow Maker!"

He watched tensely. Well he knew the power of that current! How he and Dandelion had struggled against it, trying to steer the great war canoe! But now the case was different. Arrow Maker's boat was light, his arm was strong. Seemingly without effort, he headed straight and true for All Alone Rock.

Dandelion saw him coming. He ran to the edge of the rock and stood waiting, his thin body crouched for the jump.

"He'll tip over the canoe!" cried the Captain.

"Not Dandelion!" answered Young Brave.

And he was right. The English boy did not waste his one chance. As the canoe, swerving, shot along the north face of the rock, he landed in it dead center. It scarcely rocked.

A great cheer went up from the white men. The Captain did not cheer. A big sigh of relief burst from him. But Young Brave hardly noticed. He was too busy hugging his dog.

"He's been rescued, War Cry! What now? Where will Father take him?"

That question was soon answered. Arrow Maker headed for the eastern shore.

Shouting joyously, the white soldiers ran down to meet him. Some even waded out into the water. Only the Captain and Young Brave, with the dog, remained where they were.

Arrow Maker and Dandelion sprang out, drew the canoe up on the riverbank. The soldiers crowded around them, but with a stern gesture the chief waved them back. Taking Dandelion by the hand, he walked slowly up to the Captain.

Straight and tall he stood, bearing himself with a warrior's dignity. His painted face was calm, but his dark eyes glowed in a way that showed he was deeply moved.

As for Dandelion, he looked bewildered. He was pale, and his lips trembled. Young Brave felt sorry for him. But he had no chance to greet his brother.

Already, the chief was speaking. He wasted no words. "Captain, I have two sons. One you saved from drowning. Now I bring you the other. Do you know him?"

Joy and wonder mingling in his face, the Captain gazed down at Dandelion. He said slowly, "Once I too had a son. He was blue-eyed and yellow-haired. Six years ago I lost him!"

"Six years ago," said Arrow Maker, "I took this boy into my wigwam."

"Where did you find him?"

"Over there — beyond the hills. We were raiding."

"What town?"

"How should I know? You English," said Arrow Maker, "you destroy the forest which the Great Spirit gave to us for our hunting ground. You cut down the trees, drive away the game. Then you build your stone walls along the bare earth. You give one name to one part, another name to another part. What are your names to me? All I can tell you is this, I found the child hiding in a cornfield."

"You burned the cornfield?"

"Yes. That cornfield and many others. And the house. Many houses!"

"Could the child talk when you captured him?"

"He could talk his own language. Not Algonquin. But he learned fast."

"Did he ever tell you his name?"

"Why should I ask him? My son soon gave him an Algonquin name — Dandelion, for his yellow hair."

By now, all the soldiers were gathered around the little group. They listened gravely, with puzzled faces. It was plain that they did not understand Algonquin. Turning to them, the Captain spoke rapidly in English. At once a hubbub broke out. He turned back to Arrow Maker.

"My friends tell me that I may be mistaken. They think my child is dead. But in any case this boy is English. Therefore we will take him back with us to our town."

Arrow Maker's face darkened. "No! If you are his father, I will give him to you. If not, I will keep him, for I have adopted him and he is dear to me."

"But I know he is mine!" cried the Captain. "As soon as I saw and heard him, I recognized him. Six years have passed, but he is the same boy — he is my son!"

"Then prove it!" said Arrow Maker. "Speak to him in your own language. If he is your son, he will understand you!"

The Captain's eyes flashed. "I'll do it! And he'll answer me, you'll see!" Dropping to his knees, he caught Dandelion by the shoulders. Gently, pleadingly, he began to speak in English.

Now a strange thing happened. Young Brave found himself hoping that Dandelion would answer.

"He can," he thought, "I know he can! He hasn't forgotten his own language." And he remembered the prayer-word that Dandelion had spoken in the boat, at the start of that eventful journey.

The Captain stopped, waited for an answer. No answer came. Dandelion was not even looking at him. His blue eyes, wide with panic, were fixed on Young Brave. Drops of sweat glistened on his forehead. What ailed him?

"Why, he's afraid!" thought Young Brave. "That's what's the matter with him!"

Again the Captain pleaded. Again Dandelion stood speechless. Arrow Maker watched, grim-faced. The soldiers muttered, shook their heads. At last the Captain stood up. "I was wrong," he said roughly. "He can't understand me." His eyes were wet. A warrior crying! Young Brave tried to feel scornful, but he could not.

This Englishman had become his friend. Now he was in great trouble. And what of Dandelion? It was a bad thing to lose your own people — Young Brave had found that out — but surely it was a worse thing not to know them when you found them again. Poor Dandelion! He was failing the greatest test of his life, and why was he failing? Just because he was afraid. "I can help him," thought Young Brave, "and I will!"

All these thoughts darted through his head as swiftly as mallards on the wing. Running forward, he seized Dandelion's cold hand.

"Listen to me, brother! Just now, in the war canoe, I was afraid."

"You?" gasped Dandelion.

"Yes, me! I was afraid of the Singing Water. I got over my fear, and so can you! After all, what are you afraid of? The Captain's our friend, isn't he? He saved me from Wolf Man, and afterwards he pulled me out of the whirlpool. If he's really your father, aren't you glad?"

"Well," whispered Dandelion, "perhaps I would be!"

"Then tell him who you are."

"But I don't know!"

"Don't you? I will tell you something," said Young Brave. "When you first came to live with us, you used to sit on the wigwam floor and repeat your name, with a string of other things. Over and over you said it!"

"Did I?" cried Dandelion, his eyes brightening.

"Yes, yes, you did! Now think hard! If I can remember, so can you!"

Dandelion drew a long breath. He said thoughtfully, "I sat on the wigwam floor?"

"Yes."

"Like this?" He sat down, cross-legged.

"Just like that," insisted Young Brave. But a pang shot through him.

His plan was working! And if it worked, he would lose his brother.

12

New Names

THE WATCHING MEN pressed closer. No one spoke. Everyone seemed to know that a wonderful thing was happening. The Captain's face lighted with hope.

Dandelion sat silent, a strange, faraway look shining in his blue eyes. All at once he changed. Bright rose-color swept into his pale cheeks, his eyes flashed fire. He began to speak. The English words rang out sharply: *"I am not Indian! I am English! My name —"* he hesitated, then rushed on bravely — *"is Jonathan Logan! Some day I will go home!"* He jumped up, his eyes on the Captain.

A loud, sighing murmur swelled up among the English soldiers, like a gust of wind among the pines. Some fell to their knees, some prayed as they stood. The Captain opened his arms. One spring, and Dandelion was folded close.

He was an Algonquin no more. He had found his father, his people. Beyond the hills, an English home was waiting for him.

Young Brave turned away, dashing the hot tears from his eyes. "Come, War Cry!"

But the dog hung back, eying Dandelion. He wagged his tail as if to say, "What about him?"

"Will you come on?" said the boy fiercely. "Dandelion isn't coming. He'll never hunt with us again!"

A hand fell on his shoulder. "Wait," said Arrow Maker. "Where are you going, my son?"

Young Brave could not speak.

"I am proud of you!" went on the chief. "You've acted like a good Algonquin today, and a true friend and brother. Good will come of it."

"My brother will go away," muttered the boy. "Do you call that good?"

Arrow Maker looked at him sadly. "I too will miss Dandelion in the wigwam! But you will see —"

Young Brave could listen no longer. In a minute he would be crying, and the soldiers would surely laugh at him. Shaking off his father's hand, he slipped through the crowd and walked blindly into the forest.

A familiar voice yelled, "Wait, wait for me!"

Dandelion was running after him. Young Brave stopped and waited, trying to look calm. "Well, what is it?"

"Why are you going away?" panted Dandelion. "Don't you know what you've done? Thanks to you, I've found my own father! And I have a mother too, just think! It was my mother who hid me in the corn shock when the raid began. Then she ran at top speed to get help, for my father wasn't at home. When they came back, everything was burned to the ground, and they thought I was dead. And I have a sister, a sister I've never seen! Isn't it wonderful?"

Young Brave said bitterly, "And have you a brother?"

"Only you!" said Dandelion, with a smile.

"Then you have none at all! Good-by!"

"But what is the matter with you? Of course I

must go away with my father. But I'll come back, don't you understand? I'll come back often — it's not far — and we'll hunt and fish together just as usual!"

Young Brave burst out, "You'll come back, will you? And how can you come back? Do you suppose they'll let you? Have you forgotten that your people and my people are at war?"

"Calm yourself, my boy!" said Arrow Maker, coming up behind him.

At the same moment the Captain came up behind Dandelion. Both men were smiling as they looked at each other over the heads of the excited boys.

"Did I hear your son speak of a war?" said the Captain. "As far as we English are concerned, this war is over! We've all seen a fine thing today — a friendship between an Indian boy and an English boy. If the boys can be friends, why not the fathers? What do the Indians think?"

"We Indians are ready!" answered Arrow

[139]

Maker. "But we must have our old hunting grounds back again — the land between the river and the hills. Let us move back across the river, leave us undisturbed, and never again will I lead my warriors against the towns of the English!"

"Agreed!" said the Captain heartily. "On our side, we want your trade. You have furs. We have steel axes, knives, muskets, and woolen blankets. Trade with us, and both sides will gain."

The chief's face shone with contentment. "Agreed!"

"Do you speak for your warriors?"

"I do! When I crossed the river, my warriors were already sitting in council. All were of one mind. We killed many deer today," went on Arrow Maker. "Tonight we will hold a great feast at our village in honor of the peace. Will you be our guests?"

"We will indeed!" Smiling cordially, the Captain held out his hand.

Arrow Maker hesitated. And then, with an answering smile, for the first time in his life he grasped the hand of a white man in friendship.

A glade near the village was chosen as the place for the feast. It was the same glade where Young Brave had been playing when first he sighted the English war party.

That evening, the red light of the council fire streamed far into the shadowy forest and glimmered over the dark river. There was a hum of many voices, English and Algonquin. In a great ring around the fire sat the two parties, feasting together in peace and friendship. Bright-faced Algonquin women flitted between the glade and the village, where the cooking fires burned. The evening was cool and starry. The night air smelled of pine, balsam, and cedar, of wood smoke, and roasting venison.

Up and down the riverbank, the children too were feasting.

Young Brave and Dandelion sat somewhat

apart from the others, at the foot of an old pine tree. They were sharing a venison steak. Hungry, tired, and very happy, they ate in silence.

Cricket sat close by, with her baby beaver. The beaver was asleep, and Cricket too, her meal finished, was growing drowsy. But she stayed awake in order to gaze and gaze at the two boys. Her round face beamed with contentment.

Other children were peering at the boys. Curious whispers went to and fro. Presently Keego sauntered up to them.

"What a day!" he began. "It started with war, and it ends with peace! What happened, anyway, after you two left in the war canoe?"

Young Brave made no answer.

Keego looked disappointed. "Aren't you going to tell us?"

"You didn't ask me," put in Dandelion, with a mischievous smile.

"Well, I will — I do!" cried Keego, stammer-

[142]

ing in his eagerness. "Come on, boys, Dandelion's going to tell us what happened!"

"Oh no," said Dandelion, "I'm going to tell you what *didn't* happen."

"And what was that?"

"We didn't drown ourselves!"

"Oh," muttered Keego, "I made a little mistake about that. I admit it! Now won't you tell us the story?"

But not another word could be got out of the two friends. Finally Keego went away.

"You made the peace!" said Dandelion softly.

"No," said Young Brave. "The Great Spirit made it!"

The feast went on. The English treaty was brought out and signed. The calumet went round, the sacred peace pipe, long as a boy's arm and decorated with hanging feathers and other ornaments.

There was a stir at the council fire. A drum be-

gan to beat. An Algonquin singer stepped forward
into the ring. The children came flocking up to
listen, Young Brave and Dandelion among them.
The women ran down from the village. All eyes
were on the singer.

He stamped and danced, then began to chant.
He sang of two boys, sons of enemy chiefs, launch-
ing a war canoe on a flooded river.

Young Brave started. He wanted to run away, but Dandelion held him fast by the arm. He saw his father's calm face, the dark eyes flashing proudly in the firelight. He saw his mother standing with the other women, Cricket beside her, holding up her baby beaver to listen. He saw the boys listening open-mouthed.

On and on went the song, telling of the adventures of the two boys, their perils, their friendship.

When the song ended, the oldest of the Indians raised his hand. He was Cloud Man, wrinkled of face, bright of eye. "Let my grandson come forward!"

As if in a dream, Young Brave found himself standing before the old warrior.

Cloud Man said solemnly, "Long before you were born, this war began between the Blue River Indians and the English. Now it is over! The pipe of peace has been smoked. It is a big pipe, but a small hand has filled it. Our people are saved. And it was you who saved them, by your friendship for your white brother. When friendship begins, war must end! And now I am going to give you a new name. From this day on, you shall be called Saved-His-People!"

And that is how Young Brave, as well as Dandelion, got a new name that day. It would be hard to say which boy was prouder of his new name. But still, in days to come, when they hunted and fished together, or roamed the great forest with their faithful dog War Cry, they never called each other by these wonderful new names. To one another, they were always Young Brave and Dandelion.

#369